TULSA CITY-COUNTY LIBRARY

D1608346

Smithsonian Prehistoric Zone
Tylosaurus

by Gerry Bailey
Illustrated by Karen Carr

Crabtree Publishing Company

www.crabtreebooks.com

Crabtree Publishing Company
www.crabtreebooks.com

Author
Gerry Bailey

Illustrator
Karen Carr

Editorial coordinator
Kathy Middleton

Editor
Lynn Peppas

Proofreader
Kathy Middleton

Prepress technician
Samara Parent

Print and production coordinator
Katherine Berti

Copyright © 2010 Palm Publishing LLC and the
Smithsonian Institution, Washington DC, 20560 USA
All rights reserved.

Tylosaurus, originally published as *Mosasaurus Mighty Ruler of the Sea*
by Karen Wagner, Illustrated by Karen Carr
Book copyright © 2008 Trudy Corporation and the Smithsonian
Institution, Washington DC 20560.

Library of Congress Cataloging-in-Publication Data

Bailey, Gerry.
Tylosaurus / by Gerry Bailey ; illustrated by Karen Carr.
    p. cm. -- (Smithsonian prehistoric zone)
Includes index.
ISBN 978-0-7787-1818-5 (pbk. : alk. paper) -- ISBN 978-0-7787-1805-5
(reinforced library binding : alk. paper) -- ISBN 978-1-4271-9709-2
(electronic (pdf))
1. Tylosurus--Juvenile literature. I. Carr, Karen, 1960- ill. II. Title. III.
Series.

QL638.B34B35 2011
567.9'5--dc22

                    2010044034

Library and Archives Canada Cataloguing in Publication

Bailey, Gerry
    Tylosaurus / by Gerry Bailey ; illustrated by Karen Carr.

(Smithsonian prehistoric zone)
Includes index.
At head of title: Smithsonian Institution.
Issued also in electronic format.
ISBN 978-0-7787-1805-5 (bound).--ISBN 978-0-7787-1818-5 (pbk.)

        1. Mosasauridae--Juvenile literature. I. Carr, Karen, 1960-
II. Smithsonian Institution III. Title. IV. Series: Bailey, Gerry.
Smithsonian prehistoric zone.

QE862.S65B33 2011   j567.9'5   C2010-906894-7

Crabtree Publishing Company
www.crabtreebooks.com   1-800-387-7650
Copyright © **2011 CRABTREE PUBLISHING COMPANY**.
All rights reserved. No part of this publication may be reproduced, stored in a retrieval
system or be transmitted in any form or by any means, electronic, mechanical, photocopying,
recording, or otherwise, without the prior written permission of Crabtree Publishing
Company. In Canada: we acknowledge the financial support of the Government of
Canada through the Canada Book Fund for our publishing activities.

Published in the United States
Crabtree Publishing
PMB 59051
350 Fifth Avenue, 59th Floor
New York, New York 10118

Published in Canada
Crabtree Publishing
616 Welland Ave.
St. Catharines, Ontario
L2M 5V6

Printed in China/012011/GW20101014

Dinosaurs

Living things had been around for billions of years before dinosaurs came along. Animal life on Earth started with single-cell **organisms** that lived in the seas. About 380 million years ago, some animals came out of the sea and onto the land. These were the ancestors that would become the mighty dinosaurs.

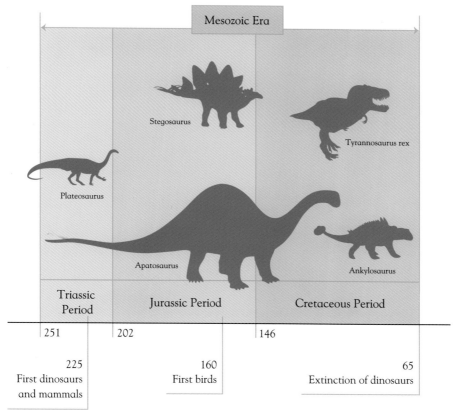

Mesozoic Era

Stegosaurus

Tyrannosaurus rex

Plateosaurus

Apatosaurus

Ankylosaurus

Triassic Period	Jurassic Period	Cretaceous Period
251	202	146

225	160	65
First dinosaurs and mammals	First birds	Extinction of dinosaurs

The dinosaur era is called the Mesozoic era. It is divided into three parts called the Triassic, Jurassic, and Cretaceous periods. During the Cretaceous period flowering plants grew for the first time and plant-eating dinosaurs, such as *Pentaceratops*, lived. Meat-eaters, such as *Tyrannosaurus rex*, fed on plant-eaters and other dinosaurs. *Pterosaurs* flew in the sky. **Marine** reptiles, such as *Tylosaurus*, swam in the seas. By the end of the Cretaceous period, the dinosaurs and most of the large air and reptiles became **extinct**.

The waves of the **prehistoric** sea broke gently on
the shore below. A herd of dinosaurs grazed on
the plants that flourished beside the forest. The
air was damp and filled with the scent of flowers.

A hungry pterosaur skimmed the surface. Its
leathery wings stretched wide and almost touched
the water. It was looking for fish to catch. It did
not see the dark shadow that appeared below.

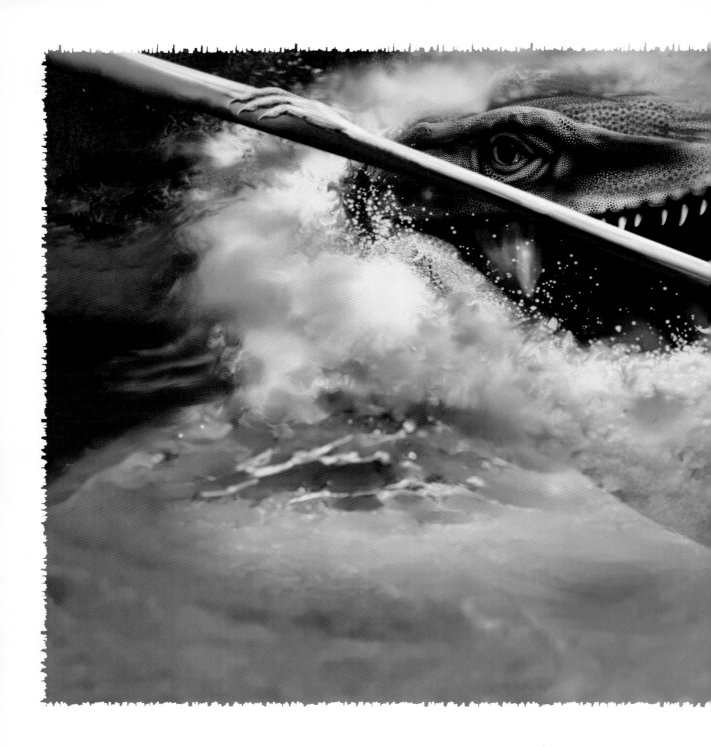

Suddenly the shadow burst into life. It was the
fearsome ruler of the seas called Tylosaurus.
Its head broke through the surface. It lunged
at the flying dinosaur with its great jaws open.

Pterosaur screamed and fled to the safety
of a birch tree. Tylosaurus was hungry.
If it had not seen him in time, Tylosaurus
would have eaten him in one huge bite.

Although he lived in water, Tylosaurus needed to breathe air. Yesterday, when he had come up to breathe he had spotted a tasty turtle warming itself on a log. He looked at the log again. This time he was not so lucky. He looked around to see if there were more turtles, but there was none. He splashed back under the warm water. He was still hungry.

Tylosaurus dived down to the seabed. He stayed very still. Above him drifted a long-necked Elasmosaurus with sharp teeth.

The prehistoric sea was a dangerous place.
Tylosaurus had learned to watch out for enemies
that also made these waters their home.

Tylosaurus could swim very well. He used his flippers to steer and his strong, streamlined body and tail to move him forward. As he glided through the seaweed, he saw another good swimmer.

It was a shark. This was not the first time Tylosaurus had seen the menacing rows of razor-sharp teeth that filled the shark's jaws. He quickly swam away and left the shark to prowl alone.

Tylosaurus spotted a rocky ledge where he might find food. Then he saw a crocodile chasing a turtle. If Tylosaurus struck now he might be lucky. The crocodile was big, but Tylosaurus had jaws that

were loosely **hinged** at the skull with a movable
joint at each side. He could open them up wide
enough to swallow large **prey**. He surged forward
and sank his teeth into the crocodile.

Tylosaurus was so busy feasting on the crocodile that he did not notice what was going on behind him. Another older Tylosaurus had spotted him. This Tylosaurus was much larger and had ferocious jaws full of sharp teeth. It was hungry, and food was food. It did not mind eating one of its own kind. But the younger one pulled his body away just in time.

The older Tylosaurus was angry, and this was its **territory**. It did not want to share its part of the sea and its food with anyone. It turned and charged once more.

18

Tylosaurus dodged but he felt the tail of his attacker wind around his own tail. He could see his enemy's white teeth ready to strike.

Finally, Tylosaurus gave a mighty twist of his tail and broke free. He had to get away, but he had been underwater for a long time. He needed to breathe air very badly. Fortunately, his enemy gave up. It was tired and swam back to its rocky ledge. Tylosaurus quickly swam up and broke through the surface. Now he could fill his lungs again. He had escaped danger.

Tylosaurus took another deep breath and plunged back into the deep. He looked for **ammonites** to eat. These were **ancient** mollusks housed in a hard, spiral shell. Tylosaurus used his strong jaws and sharp, pointed teeth to crush the shells and get at the soft meat inside. After a tough fight, Tylosaurus now had a safe place to rest and eat.

As the evening sun went down, insects buzzed around the scented, flowering trees. A three-horned Pentaceratops used its dinosaur beak

to nip off tasty ferns and munch them quietly.
Close by a sauropod reached up and plucked
the leaves from a ginkgo tree.

Tylosaurus lay quietly below the surface of the water. All was calm as night came on, but he knew that he always had to stay alert. Danger was never far away.

Tonight he was well fed. Tomorrow he would once again swim out to hunt in the seas, find food, and watch out for his enemies.

All about Tylosaurus

(TIE-luh-SORE-uss)

Tylosaurus swam between 87 and 82 million years ago in the ancient Cretaceous seas. It was not a dinosaur but an **aquatic** reptile. It shared the water with other marine reptiles, such as plesiosaurs, and fierce predator fish, such as sharks.

Precambrian Era		570 million years ago			Palaeozoic Era		
Precambrian Period		Cambrian Period	Ordovician Period	Silurian Period	Devonian Period	Carbon
				380 First life on land		First rept

Tylosaurus could reach a length of 49 feet (15 meters) or more. It could have weighed up to 7.7 tons (7 metric tons). It had a long, **cylinder**-shaped snout, which it may have used to ram or stun its prey and to fight other *Tylosaurus*. It swam using its muscular tail that had a flattened fin at the end. Four paddle-like flippers helped it steer. Although it lived in the sea, *Tylosaurus* breathed air and had to come to the surface every so often.

Tylosaurus was a deadly meat-eater, or **carnivore**. It had jaws full of sharp, cone-shaped teeth. Its prey included fish, sharks, plesiosaurs, and possibly diving birds. Some *Tylosaurus* swam in shallow waters close to shore. Some swam in deeper waters farther out to sea. Its **habitat** included an ocean that covered part of what is now North America called the Western Interior Seaway.

248

Mesozoic Era

65

Cenozoic Era

Now

Permian Period | Triassic Period | Jurassic Period | Cretaceous Period

1.8
First humans

Mosasaur family

The *Mosasaur* family lived during the late Cretaceous period. They included *Platecarpus*, *Plotosaurus*, and *Tylosaurus*. They were all powerful swimmers with streamlined bodies and short, paddle-like limbs. Their long tails made them look a little like snakes. *Mosasaurs* probably had scaly, snake-like skin.

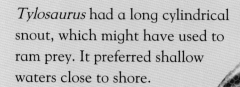

Tylosaurus had a long cylindrical snout, which might have used to ram prey. It preferred shallow waters close to shore.

Plotosaurus was the largest of the *Mosasaurs*. On the end of its tail was a **vertical** fin.

Platecarpus had a tail as long as its body with a broad fin running along its length. It used its fins to steer like *Tylosaurus*.

Present-day animal

Monitor Lizard This lizard is related to the *Mosasaur* family.

Glossary

ammonites Large, spiral-shelled mollusks that lived during the Mesozoic era

ancient A very long time ago

aquatic Living in water

carnivore An animal that eats the flesh of other animals

cylinder A round, hollow shape, such as a pipe

extinct No longer living on Earth

habitat A natural place where an animal lives

hinge A joint that lets something open and close

joint Bones that fit together, such as elbow, to allow motion

marine Related to the ocean

organism Any living thing, such as an animal or plant

prehistoric Before the time when events were recorded by humans

prey An animal that is hunted by another

territory An area of land

vertical In a straight up and down direction

Index

Further Reading and Websites

Ocean Monsters by Natalie Lunis. Bearport Publishing (2008)

Giant Sea Reptiles of the Dinosaur Age by Caroline Arnold. Clarion (2007)

Websites:

www.smithsonianeducation.org